Would you rather...

John Burningham

RED FOX

Other books by John Burningham

Aldo

Avocado Baby

Borka

Cloudland

Come away from the water, Shirley

Courtney

Granpa

Harquin

Humbert

Husherbye

John Patrick Norman McHennessy

The Magic Bed

Mr Gumpy's Motor Car

Mr Gumpy's Outing

Oi! Get off our Train

The Shopping Basket

Simp

Time to get out of the bath, Shirley

Trubloff

Whadaymean

Where's Julius?

BRENT LIBRARIES	
91120000329088	
Askews & Holts	31-May-2017
	£7.99

WOULD YOU RATHER . . .
A RED FOX BOOK 978 0 099 20041 3

First published in Great Britain by Jonathan Cape,
an imprint of Random House Children's Publishers UK

Jonathan Cape edition published 1978
This Red Fox edition published 1999

27 29 30 28 26

Copyright © John Burningham, 1978

The right of John Burningham to be identified as the author of this work has been
asserted in accordance with the Copyright, Designs and Patents Act 1988.

All rights reserved. No part of this publication may be reproduced, stored in a retrieval system,
or transmitted in any form or by any means, electronic, mechanical, photocopying,
recording or otherwise, without the prior permission of the publishers.

Red Fox books are published by Random House Children's Publishers UK,
a division of the Random House Group Ltd, London, Sydney,
Auckland, Johannesburg and agencies throughout the world.

THE RANDOM HOUSE GROUP Limited Reg. No. 954009
www.randomhousechildrens.co.uk

A CIP catalogue record for this book is available from the British Library.

Printed in China by Tien Wah Press Sdn Bhd

Would you rather . . .

your house was surrounded by

water

snow

or jungle

Would you rather . . .

an elephant drank your bath water

an eagle
stole your dinner

a pig tried on your clothes

or a hippo slept in your bed

Would you rather be . . .

covered in jam

soaked
with water

or pulled through the mud by a dog

Would you rather have . . .

supper in a castle   breakfast in a balloon

or tea on the river

Would you rather be made to eat . . .

spider stew

slug dumplings

mashed
worms

or
drink
snail
squash

Would you rather . . .

jump in the nettles for £5

swallow a dead frog for £20

or stay all night in a creepy house for £50

Would you rather be . . .

crushed by a snake

swallowed by a fish

eaten by a crocodile

or sat on by a rhinoceros

Would you rather . . .

your dad did a dance at school

or your mum had a row in a cafe

Would you rather . . .

clash the cymbals

bang the drum

or blow the trumpet

Would you rather have . . .

a monkey to tickle

a bear to read to

a cat to box with

a dog to skate with

a pig to ride

or a goat to dance with

Would you rather be chased by . . .

a crab

a bull

a lion

or wolves

Or would you like to ride a bull
into a supermarket

Would you rather be lost . . .

in the fog

at sea

in a desert

in a forest

or in a crowd

Would you rather help . . .

a fairy make magic   gnomes dig for treasure

an imp be naughty

a witch make a stew

or Santa Claus deliver presents

Would you rather live with . . .

a gerbil in a cage

a fish in a bowl

a parrot on a perch

a rabbit in a hutch

chickens in a coop

or a dog in a kennel

Or perhaps you would rather
just go to sleep in your own bed